Floppy Friends
GO TO
CAMP

by
Nancy E. Krulik

ISBN 0-439-08378-8

Published by Scholastic Inc.

12 11 10 9 8 7 6 5 4 3 2 1   9/9 0 1 2 3 4/0

Designed by Joan Ferrigno

Printed in the U.S.A.   14

First Scholastic printing, July 1999

Floppy Friends
GO TO CAMP

by
Nancy E. Krulik

SCHOLASTIC INC.
New York   Toronto   London   Auckland   Sydney
Mexico City   New Delhi   Hong Kong

CHAPTER one
WELCOME, CAMPERS

"We're here because we're here, because we're here, because we're here, because we're here. . . ."

The kids on the yellow school bus began singing louder and louder as the signs for Camp Thunder Hill appeared along the highway. Hooray! They were almost there!

"Look! There's Carly's Candy Store," Prince croaked as the bus passed by a small shop with a penny candy sign in the window. "I hope we get to hike there this year. My mom sent me to camp with a five-dollar bill. I can buy 500 pieces of penny candy with that!"

Prince's best friend, Moe, stuck his head out of the bus window and tried to peer into the woods. "Ooo, ooo, ooo!" the monkey exclaimed as he spotted a small wooden tent. "I think I see the lean-to we built last summer. I'm really glad they didn't take it down."

As the other campers happily traded memories from last summer, Dot sat quietly in her seat. A small tear streamed down the little ladybug's tiny face. This was Dot's very first summer away from home. She didn't know anyone at camp. Everyone else seemed to know one another. It was horrible being the only new camper.

But Dot was wrong. She was not the only new camper. Buster, the big, gruff bulldog in the back of the bus, was new, too. But he wasn't crying. He was too busy bragging.

"You call that a lean-to?" Buster boasted. "At my old camp we built tree houses. They were fifty feet off the ground! Now that's cool."

The other campers didn't respond. They were too busy cheering. The bus had just rounded a corner and driven up a hill. They had arrived!

Suddenly Honey pounded her fists on the seat. The other campers followed her lead. Soon the pounding sounded like a powerful thunderstorm. The kids broke into their camp cheer.

"Thunder Hill is our name. Having fun is why we came! Swimming, boating, softball, too. There's no end to what we can do. One, two, three, four, five. We're not gonna take no jive. Six, seven, eight, nine, ten. Back it up and start again."

As the campers began the cheer again, Dot tried to join in. But her tongue got all twisted as the kids sang faster and faster. She felt another tear drip down the side of her face.

Buster wasn't singing the camp cheer, either. He was shouting over the voices of the other campers. "You guys want to hear a real cheer?" he growled. "Try this one. I go to Thunder Hill so pity me. There's not a decent girl in the vicinity. And every night at nine they lock the doors. I don't know what I ever came here for. . . . "

Honey turned around and put a furry bear paw over Buster's mouth. "That's not nice," she told him angrily. "I don't know what your old camp was like, but we have camp spirit here."

Buster shook his face free. Then he frowned and looked out the window. The counselors were running up to the bus with clipboards in hand. A tall man with a thick bushy beard and stringy blond hair bounded up the stairs of the bus.

"Welcome, campers! I'm Eddie Spaghetti, the head counselor at Camp Thunder Hill," he introduced himself. "Are you guys ready to have fun this summer?"

"Oh, yeah!" all the campers shouted out. (Well, all the campers except Buster. He just groaned.)

"Great!" Eddie Spaghetti exclaimed. "Now, when you hear your name, step off the bus, and one of

our amazing counselors will show you to your cabin."

As Dot waited for her name to be called, she looked out at the camp. It seemed so big. There was a giant green field surrounded by wooden cabins. Through the trees, she could see a bright blue lake on the other side of a hill. There were also tennis courts and a baseball diamond nearby.

"Moe and Prince, you two are together again," Eddie Spaghetti said. "Cabin 12 this time. Buster, that's your cabin, too."

The boys got off the bus. "You want us to show you where Cabin 12 is?" Moe asked Buster.

Buster shook his head. "How hard can it be to find Cabin 12? It's got to be right next to Cabin 11, right?" But he followed close behind Moe and Prince anyway.

"Honey, you're in Cabin 1 — the oldest girls," Eddie Spaghetti said with a smile. "And Dot, you're in Cabin 1, too."

Dot looked around at all the cabins. She figured number 1 would be the first cabin.

But she couldn't tell where the line of cabins began and where it ended.

"Come on, I'll show you the way," Honey said sweetly.

By the time Dot and Honey reached the cabin, almost all of the beds had been taken. The campers were busy putting their clothes in their cubbies and hanging pictures on the wall. The only two beds left were a pair of bunk beds by the window.

"Is it okay with you if I take the top one?" Dot asked shyly.

"Fine with me," Honey said with a smile.

Suddenly a loud voice boomed out through the loudspeakers. "Attention, campers! Lunch is now being served in the mess hall!"

"Come on, Dot," Honey called to her new friend. "Let's hurry. I want to find a seat near Moe and Prince. I hope we're having sloppy joes today!"

Dot gulped. Sloppy joes in a mess hall. Dot was actually a pretty neat eater. Was she ever going to fit in at Camp Thunder Hill?

CHAPTER two
BUG JUICE AND SALT SHAKERS

Dot was relieved when she saw that the mess hall was really just a big cafeteria — like the one at her school. There were rows and rows of tables with benches. Kids with trays were lined up, waiting for their meat sandwiches and tomato soup.

"Hey, Honey, we're over here," Moe called out from a table near the back.

Honey nodded. "Let's go sit with Moe and Prince," she suggested to Dot as she picked up her food and carried the tray toward the back of the room.

Just as Dot and Honey took their places at the table, Buster came over. "This food stinks," he complained. "At my old camp we had Belgian waffles for lunch — with whipped cream!"

Dot doubted that was true, but she didn't say anything. Instead she reached for a pitcher that was sitting on the table. She poured some bright red liquid into her cup.

"What's this?" Dot asked Honey.

13

"Bug juice," Buster answered before Honey could say anything. "Red blood squeezed fresh from bugs!"

Bug blood! The little ladybug gasped.

"Cut it out, Buster," Honey scolded the bulldog.

"It's not bug blood," Moe assured Dot. "It's just fruit punch. They only call it bug juice."

Dot breathed a sigh of relief. But she waited to see if everyone else drank it, just in case.

"We have a swim test after rest hour," Prince said. "I hope I pass the test to go down the water slide."

"I'd like that, too," sighed Honey. "But I'm such a lousy swimmer."

Moe patted her on the back. "Come on, last year you started out being afraid to even go in the water. By the end of the summer, you were kicking your feet and swimming with a kickboard. That's real progress!"

Moe took a spoonful of soup and looked over at Buster. "Pass the salt, will you, Buster?" he asked. "This stuff needs a little spice."

"Sure thing, buddy," Buster said. He calmly pushed the shaker across the table.

Moe tipped the shaker over his soup. The top popped off the shaker. SPLAT! A huge pile of salt landed in the middle of Moe's soup.

Buster began laughing hysterically. "Gotcha!" he screamed.

"That's not funny," the monkey muttered. "I can't eat this. Now I'll have to wait in line for another bowl!" He got up and went back in line.

"What's wrong with him?" Buster said. "Can't he take a little joke?"

"That's not a joke," Honey replied angrily.

"Boy, this camp is no fun at all," Buster complained. "At my old camp we played jokes on each other all the time. I remember once when . . ."

"Why don't you just go back to your old camp?" Prince shouted at Buster. Then he hopped up from the bench and moved to another table. Honey and Dot followed close behind him.

Buster laughed out loud as he watched them leave. "Good!" he called after them. "Now all the bug juice is for me!"

CHAPTER three
The Missing Maniac

It took a few days, but eventually Dot began to feel at home at Camp Thunder Hill. She'd already made three new friends — Honey, Moe, and Prince. In arts and crafts she'd learned to do the butterfly stitch and the box stitch to make a lanyard necklace. She'd done so well on her swimming test that she was allowed to swim in the deep water with Moe and Prince. And even though Honey had only been able to swim a little, she did well enough to be allowed to go canoeing — with a life jacket on, of course.

So as the campers settled down to enjoy their first campfire, Dot was relaxed. Prince volunteered to show her how to toast marshmallows.

Dot carefully pushed her marshmallow onto a long stick and held it over the coals. When it was gently browned, Dot lifted the marshmallow from the fire and slid it into her mouth. Mmmm. It was delicious — warm and crispy on the outside; cool and mushy on the inside.

After a while, the counselors stood. It was time to go back to the cabins. But Buster stopped them.

"I can't believe you guys," he complained. "What kind of wimpy campfire is this? We haven't heard one ghost story!"

"Yeah! Yeah! Yeah!" Moe agreed enthusiastically. "I love a good, scary story!"

"Me too!" Prince agreed. "Do you know any?"

Buster stood up proudly. "Only the scariest one of all," he declared. "I learned it in my old camp!"

Honey rolled her eyes at Dot, but the girls sat down to hear the story anyway.

"It's called the Missing Maniac," Buster said. "Once there was a boy who went to a camp right here in these mountains. He was ugly, with a red, red face and bulging eyes. The other kids laughed at him. They made him feel so bad that he ran off into the woods alone one night. The woods were dark and creepy, and the trees blocked all of his paths. He couldn't find his way back to the camp. The next day, when the counselors realized the boy was missing, they sent the police to look for him. But they never found him.

People say he still roams these woods. Every summer, he captures one camper and holds him prisoner forever — that's how he takes his revenge on the campers who forced him to hide in the woods! Beware! This year it could be you!"

Dot had trouble falling asleep that night. The day had been so exciting, and she was a little shaken by Buster's tale. As the other girls in her cabin drifted off, Dot heard a rustling in the leaves outside the cabin door.

"Honey! Honey! Wake up!" Dot cried out. She hung over the side of her bed. "I hear someone in the woods. Maybe it's the Missing Maniac!"

Honey opened her weary eyes and looked up at Dot's frightened face. "There's no Missing Maniac. You probably heard a squirrel or something."

Dot lay back down. But as she turned toward the window she saw a face staring at her — a scary face with glowing eyes and red skin.

"AAAAAHHH!" Dot cried out. "It's a monster! It's the maniac!"

Suddenly the face disappeared. Dot heard laughter outside her window.

"I'd know that laugh anywhere!" Honey declared. "Come on, Dot!"

But Dot was too scared to move. Honey went outside the cabin on her own.

"I thought it was you, Buster," she said, coming face-to-face with the bulldog.

Buster frowned. "What's the big deal? All I did was shine my flashlight under my chin like this," he said as he placed his flashlight under his face. The light gave his face a creepy red glow. "It was just a joke."

"We're all getting sick of your jokes!" Honey declared. As she turned and went back into her cabin, Honey let the door slam loudly.

CHAPTER four
SPLASH!

The next afternoon, Dot and Honey took their first canoe ride on the lake. Honey sat in the back and steered, while Dot sat up front.

"Dot, will you be my partner on the canoe trip?" Honey asked her new friend. "I'm a little afraid of going down the river. Last summer, I was so afraid that a counselor had to go in my canoe with me."

Dot smiled. She knew what it was like to need a friend when you were afraid. "You bet!" Dot agreed happily. "I can't wait for this trip. I've never been canoeing on a river before. And I've never slept outside under the stars before, either!"

Just then Prince swam over and sat on a lily pad close to the canoe. "Wait until you see the mud slide!" he said. "It's really slick, and you get so muddy!"

"The canoe trip is the best!" Moe agreed from his perch on a branch that overlooked the water.

"Hey, you guys, check this out!" Buster called out over the lake. The other campers looked up just in time to see Buster cannonball off the diving board.

SPLASH! Buster's dive was so powerful, it rocked the canoe. Honey gasped. She was afraid of falling in. Luckily the canoe righted itself quickly.

But Buster had seen the canoe rocking back and forth. That gave him an idea. He swam underwater until he reached the canoe. Then he popped up right behind Honey and shouted out, "BOO!"

Honey was startled. She jumped up without thinking. The canoe flopped on its side, throwing Honey and Dot into the water.

Even though she had her life jacket on, Honey started to panic. She'd never been in deep water before. Her arms and legs flailed wildly.

"Hold on to the canoe," Dot told her friend. "Just lean your body over and hold on." As Honey grabbed the canoe, Dot called over to Moe and Prince. "You guys get help, quickly!" she ordered.

Moe grabbed onto a nearby rope swing and swung like Tarzan over the lake. Prince swam for the dock. They called over to a lifeguard. The lifeguard dove into the water and swam over to the girls. He showed them how to right the canoe and climb back in. Then he helped Dot and Honey row back to shore.

"Are you all right?" the lifeguard asked Honey as they put the canoe away.

"I think so," Honey said. "I'm just glad Dot was there to calm me down."

"And I'll be there the whole time we're on the canoe trip," Dot assured Honey.

The next morning, all of the campers met by the waterfront. It was time to load up the canoes and move on down the river.

"You shouldn't even be allowed to go after what you did to Honey yesterday," Dot said to Buster.

"Fine with me." Buster shrugged. "A canoe trip sounds pretty stupid, anyway."

"At least Buster will be in a canoe with one of the counselors," Honey told Moe.

Moe looked over as Buster put his knapsack into his canoe. "He's been quiet all morning," Moe replied. "He hasn't said a word to anyone. I wonder what he's up to."

"Probably nothing good," Honey said.

The boating counselor helped Buster into the first canoe. The others lined up behind him. "Let's go!" the counselor called out. "We want to hit those mud slides before lunch!"

CHAPTER five
A NOISE IN THE NIGHT

The kids had a great time canoeing down the river. They splashed, laughed, and sang every camp song they had ever heard. Finally the camp counselors motioned for the campers to dock their canoes near a big muddy hill.

"MUD SLIDE!" Moe shouted as he leaped out of his canoe, scrambled up the side of the hill, and slid down the mud at top speed. He landed in the river with a big muddy splash.

"Hey! Wait for me!" Prince croaked as he, too, slid down the slippery slope.

Soon all of the kids were covered in mud. All of the kids except Buster.

"I am the Mud Monster," Prince said in his deepest Frankenstein voice. He was covered in mud and walking like a monster over toward Buster.

"Cut that out!" Buster said.

"Why aren't you sliding with us?" Prince asked.

"It's more fun watching you guys make fools of yourselves," Buster snapped back.

Prince just shrugged and went back to play in the mud.

After a while, the kids rinsed off in the river and went up the hill to set up their campsite. They put up their tents, lay out their sleeping bags, and set up a big circle of rocks where the fire would be. Then they broke into teams and went to look for firewood.

"Hey, Buster, aren't you going to help us look for wood?" Honey asked.

Buster shook his head. "I'm going to stay here and guard the food," he said.

Moe laughed. "We're the only ones here. Who are you guarding it from — the Missing Maniac?"

The other kids laughed, but Buster stayed put.

That night, the kids built a giant campfire. They cooked hot dogs and hamburgers over the flames, and toasted marshmallows. The boating counselor told them stories about the Native Americans who had lived in the mountains. Finally it was time to go to sleep. Like all of the other kids, Dot and Honey went into their tent and zipped themselves into their sleeping bags. It had been a long, long day. Within minutes the giggling from inside the tents stopped. Everyone was asleep.

Dot wasn't sure how long she had been asleep when she heard a noise outside her tent. At first, Dot was frightened. What if this time it really was the Missing Maniac, or some other monster that lived in the woods?

But after listening for a few seconds, Dot realized she wasn't hearing monster noises at all. They were soft, muffled sobs. Somebody out there was crying.

Dot unzipped her sleeping bag and snuck out of the tent, trying hard not to wake Honey. She walked out into the campsite. There, by the fire, Dot saw something she never dreamed she would ever see. It was Buster. He was sitting all hunched over, crying.

"Hey, Buster, what's wrong? Why are you crying?" Dot whispered.

Buster rubbed his eyes quickly. "Me? I'm not crying. It's just the smoke. It got in my eyes."

Dot knew he was lying, but she didn't want to embarrass him. "Okay," she said. She started walking back toward her tent.

"Hey, Dot?" Buster whispered. "Wanna hang out for a while?"

Dot looked at Buster. He didn't seem to be joking this time. He seemed to need a friend.

"Sure," Dot replied. She sat down next to him. "Why are you out here instead of in your tent?"

Buster looked down at his feet. "Promise not to tell?" he asked her. "I'm scared," the bulldog admitted finally. "I've never slept out in the woods before."

"But what about at your old camp?" Dot asked.

Buster frowned. "They had their camp-out at the end of the summer," he said simply.

"So?" Dot asked.

"I didn't stay that long," Buster whispered. "I got homesick after just two weeks. I went home."

For a few minutes neither of them talked. Dot now understood why Buster had acted so tough. He was scared and homesick, just like he had been at his old camp. He just didn't want anyone to know.

"You promised not to tell," Buster reminded her.

Dot nodded. "I have a great idea. Let's stay up all night. We'll hang out together by the fire, okay?"

Buster smiled for the first time all day. "Hey, you want to learn a neat trick?" he asked Dot. He pulled the hood of his sweatshirt onto his head. Then he pulled the strings really, really tight until only his

nose was showing.

"That's funny," Dot giggled. "You look like you have no face."

The next morning, Dot and Buster showed everyone how to look like faceless monsters. Everyone loved Buster's new trick. This one was funny — not mean.

As the kids began packing up their bags, Honey walked over toward Dot.

"Would you be angry if I went with the boating counselor on the way back?" Honey asked her pal. "I'm still a little afraid."

Dot shook her head. "I think that's a great idea," Dot told Honey. "I'll ride with Buster instead."

On the way back to camp, the boating counselor and Honey stayed at the end of the line of canoes, just so the counselor could keep an eye on everyone else. Dot and Buster volunteered to lead the way back to camp. As they paddled along, Buster and Dot started cheering.

"Thunder Hill is our name. Having fun is why we came! Swimming, boating, softball, too. There's no end to what we can do!"

Dot reached up and gave Buster a big high five. They weren't the new kids anymore. They were just Thunder Hill campers, like everyone else. And that was so cool!